DOGGONE...
THIRD
GRADE!

DOGGONE.... THIRD GRADE!

by COLLEEN O'SHAUGHNESSY McKENNA

illustrated by STEPHANIE ROTH

SCHOLASTIC INC.
New York   Toronto   London   Auckland   Sydney
Mexico City   New Delhi   Hong Kong   Buenos Aires

ISBN 0-439-56710-6

Text copyright © 2002 by Colleen O'Shaughnessy McKenna.
Illustrations copyright © 2002 by Stephanie Roth. All rights reserved. Published by Scholastic Inc., 557 Broadway, New York, NY 10012, by arrangement with Holiday House, Inc.
SCHOLASTIC and associated logos are trademarks and/or registered trademarks of Scholastic Inc.

12 11 10 9   8/0

Printed in the U.S.A.   40

First Scholastic printing, December 2003

To my much-loved friend, Sally Alexander,
and the memory of her dog Ursula,
who guided her so well.
C. O. M.

To Matthew Baker,
amazing friend.
S. R.

Chapter
1

"I want to stay in third grade forever, Lamont," Gordie said to his best friend. "Even when I'm fifty."

"Me too," Lamont said. "We'll be old enough to drive to school then."

"We can be bus drivers!" Gordie said. "We'll give candy to all the kids on our bus!"

Lamont scrambled out of his seat. "Cool! We'll let dogs ride our bus."

"We'll make them bus patrol dogs!"

Lamont and Gordie slapped high five.

The first bell rang and Miss Tingle flashed the lights. That's what she did to make the kids in room 9 sit down and stop talking. Flashing lights was a lot nicer than yelling.

"I have some exciting news for room nine," Miss Tingle said.

"Yippee, pizza for lunch!" cried Gordie.

Miss Tingle laughed. "Better than pizza, Gordie. Our class is going to have a talent show."

A few kids clapped. Lucy stood up and waved her hand. "Oh, oh, Miss Tingle! I was in a talent show this summer at my uncle's bowling alley. I sang two songs and then I did cartwheels all the way down the alley."

Gordie frowned. Lucy was always bragging about something. He had to share a locker with her. He wanted to share with Lamont. Lamont never bragged.

"And, I can even draw pictures with my eyes closed." Lucy drew in a deep breath and sat down. She popped right back up again. "Plus, I can play the piano . . . sort of."

"I can play the piano with both hands," called out Mikey.

Miss Tingle smiled. "That's wonderful. I'm sure each child in room nine has a very interesting talent."

Lucy waved her hand. "I have the most talents, Miss Tingle. Maybe I should take *two* turns in the show."

Gordie poked Lamont in the arm. "Do you think she can make herself disappear?"

Lamont laughed. "Presto, no more Lucy!"

Miss Tingle frowned. "Boys, do you have something to say?"

Gordie sat up straighter. "No, Miss Tingle." Miss Tingle didn't like anyone to be mean. She said room 9 was one big happy family. But Gordie didn't feel like Lucy was a sister. Mostly he thought of her as a pain in the neck.

Miss Tingle smiled at Gordie. She never stayed mad. Not even when Joey Martin threw up in her trash can.

Lamont raised his hand. "My uncle has a talent."

"What is his talent?" asked Miss Tingle.

"He can make a jar of pickles disappear!"

"How does he make the pickles disappear?" Miss Tingle asked.

"He eats them!" Lamont said.

Everyone laughed. Miss Tingle shook her head and grinned.

"That's not a talent!" snapped Lucy. "It's called *eating*."

Lamont waved his hand. "And, my uncle Herbie knows how to swallow snakes."

Gordie shuddered. He'd met Uncle Herbie once. He was as big as a tree. His hands were the size of dinner plates.

"I bet you're lying." Lucy got out of her seat and stared at Lamont. "Nobody eats snakes, Lamont."

Lamont grinned. "What about candy gummy snakes?"

Miss Tingle clapped her hands. Gordie saw that she wasn't smiling so much anymore. "We only have a few days to put together the show, so let's start planning."

Lamont raised his hand again. "Miss Tingle, call on me."

Miss Tingle smiled at Lamont. "Is this a *real* talent, Lamont?"

Lamont nodded. "I can play the guitar. My brother taught me this summer."

Miss Tingle got out a piece of chalk. "Let's list room nine's talents."

More and more kids raised their hands. Miss Tingle's list got longer and longer. Miss Tingle's chalk got shorter and shorter.

Gordie looked at the list. He wanted his name on the board. But, he didn't know how to sing or dance. He didn't know how to play the piano. He couldn't draw very well. All his animals looked like cats. Even his cows looked like cats.

After ten minutes, Miss Tingle put down the chalk. "Have we heard from everyone?"

"You haven't heard from Gordie!" Lucy called out.

Gordie slumped deeper into his seat. Lucy sure had a big mouth. She had the biggest mouth in the whole school.

"Gordie, what are you going to do for the show?" Miss Tingle asked gently.

Gordie shrugged. "I don't know yet." He bit his lip. "I can ride a two-wheeler. With no hands."

"So can everyone in the whole wide world," said Lucy. "That doesn't count,

Gordie. Plus, there are too many desks in here. You'd ride into the fish tank."

"Ha, ha, very funny," mumbled Gordie. He stared at his desk while a few kids laughed. Lamont reached over and patted his arm.

"Would you like to do something else, Gordie?" asked Miss Tingle.

Gordie sat up straighter. "I know how to spell lots of words."

Lucy flipped her hair over her shoulders. "Boring!"

Miss Tingle snapped her fingers. "That's enough, Lucy."

Lucy pretended she was looking for something in her desk. Nobody liked to be yelled at by Miss Tingle. Lucy popped her head out of her desk. "Gordie can have one of my talents."

Miss Tingle smiled. "That's nice to share, Lucy. But I'm sure Gordie has his own talent."

"Yeah," said Gordie. But his voice wasn't very loud.

"He has lots of them," said Lamont. "Real good ones."

"Great," said Miss Tingle. "Can I write one down?"

Gordie had a great idea. "I know. I'll be the audience."

Everyone laughed. Miss Tingle smiled. "We're inviting Mr. Johnson's class to watch our show."

"What?" Gordie thumped his head down on his desk.

"Cool," said Lucy. "The big kids are coming."

"Is everything okay, Gordie?" asked Miss Tingle.

"No," Gordie mumbled. Two things were very wrong. First of all, he didn't have a talent. Second of all, his big brother, Doug, was in Mr. Johnson's room. Doug and all his friends would boo Gordie for not having a talent.

Gordie raised his hand to ask Miss Tingle if he could go lie down on the nurse's couch. Maybe he could catch some germs there. He was busy waving his hand when someone knocked on the door.

Chapter 2

Everyone turned and watched Miss Tingle open the door. The principal, Mr. Fratorolli, walked in. A tall boy with bright orange hair followed him.

"Good morning, Miss Tingle. Good morning, class," said Mr. Fratorolli. "I have a special surprise for you this morning."

"This must be Richard Jenkins," said Miss Tingle. She reached out her hand and Richard shook it. "Welcome to room nine, Richard."

"Richard prefers to be called Red," said Mr. Fratorolli. He handed Miss Tingle some papers and waved good-bye.

Gordie stared at Red. He wished he had a cool nickname. His brother called him

Shrimp, but Gordie didn't want other people calling him that, especially since he was the shortest kid in room 9. Red's hair was the nice orange color of a new basketball.

"I know you will enjoy meeting the children in this school," said Miss Tingle. "Why don't you sit in front of Lamont? Lamont, raise your hand."

Red nodded. He kept his eyes on the floor as he walked down the aisle. His cheeks were getting pink and he kept swallowing. Gordie decided to tell Red at lunch that kids were only staring because their school didn't get many new kids. They weren't staring because of his hair.

"Boy, you sure have bright hair," said Lucy.

"Lucy," snapped Miss Tingle.

Lucy looked surprised. "I'm not being rude. He has great hair, kind of like it's plugged into electricity. My aunt Loretta has red hair and that's why she gets to do commercials on TV. She sells salad dressing and mouthwash."

"That's enough, Lucy," said Miss Tingle.

Red smiled. "That's okay. I do commercials, too."

Gordie leaned closer. The new kid was on TV?

"You do commercials for television?" asked Miss Tingle.

Red looked up. "Well, not me, but my dog, Lawrence, does commercials. He sells dog food and flea shampoo."

"Cool!" cried Lucy. "Bring your dog to school and he can be in our talent show."

Lucy added, "He can have Gordie's turn in the show. He doesn't have a talent."

"Lucy—" began Miss Tingle.

"I do, too," said Gordie. "And *my* dog has a talent, too."

Lamont stared at Gordie. "Scratch knows tricks?"

"Yeah," said Gordie. He felt bad lying to his best friend, but the whole class was looking at him. Scratch didn't even know how to roll over.

"Oh, yeah?" said Lucy. "Well, I saw your dog when I went trick-or-treating and he looked pretty dumb to me. In fact, he hid

under your porch when a ghost came up and said, 'Trick or treat.'"

"Sit down, Lucy," said Miss Tingle. "Gordie will decide on his talent when he is ready." She checked her watch. "We had better take out our spellers or we'll be late for lunch."

Lamont raised his hand. "Miss Tingle?"

"Yes, Lamont?"

Gordie sat up straight and smiled.

Lamont was probably going to tell Miss Tingle to throw Lucy out of third grade for having such a big mouth.

But Lamont said, "Red can eat lunch with me. I can show him around the school so he won't get lost."

"How nice of you, Lamont," said Miss Tingle.

Gordie nodded. He'd help show Red around, too. He could take him upstairs and show him all the fifth-graders.

The room got noisy as desk tops went up and spelling books were slapped on the desks. Mikey and Lucy raced up to sharpen their pencils. Lucy always had to be first in line, even for pencil-sharpening.

"Lamont," whispered Gordie.

But Lamont was already out of his seat, asking Miss Tingle for a speller for Red. Miss Tingle got one from the cupboard and smiled at him.

Gordie tried to grab Lamont's arm as he raced past. But then he was busy giving Red his special pencil, the one he'd gotten at Disney World.

"Thanks," said Red. "I'll give it back tomorrow."

Lamont loved that pencil so much, Gordie had never even asked to borrow it. Or touch it.

"That's okay," said Lamont. "You can just keep it."

Gordie's mouth fell open, then clamped together hard as Lamont and Red smiled and gave each other high fives.

Gordie opened his speller and tried not to watch Lamont and Red. But it was hard.

14

Gordie was so busy staring at them that he didn't hear Miss Tingle call on him. He was so busy staring at them that he didn't hear the lunch bell ring.

"Gordie, wake up," said Lamont.

Gordie closed his speller and got in line behind Lamont and Red. Lamont was so busy telling Red about the talent show that he didn't even notice when Gordie stopped to tie his shoe. He just kept laughing and walking down the stairs to the cafeteria.

Gordie took his time tying his sneaker. Then he opened his locker and stared at his jacket. Finally he walked over and took a long, long drink from the water fountain. The hall was empty. Nobody even knew he wasn't in the cafeteria. Lamont was probably asking Red if he wanted half of his sandwich.

What was so special about Red anyway? Big, big deal that Red's dog was on TV. Gordie headed down the hall, wishing Scratch could be a little bit more fancy—fancy enough to get Lamont back as a best friend.

Chapter
3

By the time Gordie got down to the cafeteria everyone was already eating lunch.
Gordie squeezed in beside Lamont, but
there wasn't much room since everyone
was gathered around Red like he was a
movie star. Gordie opened his lunch bag
and grabbed his sandwich so hard his fingers dug into the peanut butter.

Lamont was ordering kids around. "Hey,
move back, guys. Give Red some room."
Lamont wiggled on the bench and almost
shoved Gordie onto the floor. "Can't you
see he's trying to eat?"

Gordie shoved his sandwich back into
the bag. Lamont was acting like he was a
cafeteria lady.

Lucy rolled a meatball down the table. "Here, Red. You can give this to your dog."

"You have to bring your dog to school," said Mikey. "It would make room nine kind of famous."

"Dogs aren't allowed in the school," said Gordie. "Miss Tingle would get fired. Is that what you guys want?"

Lamont didn't even answer Gordie. He started telling Red that he could play the guitar. Gordie knew Lamont didn't really know how to play. Nobody could tell which song it was. All his songs sounded like "Three Blind Mice."

Gordie's stomach was doing jumping jacks. He didn't have a talent. His dog didn't have a talent. It didn't seem fair.

"I'm going to float a paper clip on water," said Jeremy.

"That's a good trick," said Lucy. "What kind of trick is your scaredy-cat dog going to do, Gordie? Maybe he could hide his head in Miss Tingle's trash can."

"Oh, be quiet," said Lamont. He leaned

18

over and bumped his shoulder against Gordie's. "Scratch is ten times smarter than you."

Lucy closed her eyes. "Fine, show me."

"He will," snapped Lamont. "Maybe Gordie and Red will have their dogs do a trick together, right, Gordie?"

Red nodded. "My dog knows how to jump over barrels and walk backward. But he can't bark to ten or anything like that."

Gordie wished Scratch could count to ten. He wished his dog knew so much math that they'd be the hit of the talent show. He looked up. Everyone was staring at him, waiting for him to prove that Scratch wasn't just a dumb dog. Lamont elbowed him.

"So, what kind of trick can Scratch do, Gordie? Can he bark to three or four?"

Gordie tried to swallow. "Well . . ."

"See," said Lucy. "I told you."

Gordie crinkled up his lunch bag and stood up. "Scratch knows how to do something real hard, Lucy Diaz."

"Like what?" asked Lucy.

"Yeah, tell her, Gordie," said Lamont.

Gordie took a deep breath. "He knows how to count, how to add, how to subtract, and—"

Gordie never got a chance to finish. Everyone was too busy laughing at him, even Lamont.

Chapter
4

As soon as Gordie and Lamont reached the playground, Lamont said, "Don't be mad at me. I didn't mean to laugh at you. But we both know Scratch can't do tricks."

"I know," Gordie said slowly. Scratch didn't even know how to bury a bone. "I'll teach him some tricks real fast."

Lamont nodded. "I'll see if I can come over and help you."

Lucy and Melinda Jones raced over. "Tell Melinda about your dog, Gordie. She doesn't believe you one bit."

Melinda was a fourth-grader who was pretty mean to everyone. Even some of the sixth-grade boys were afraid of her.

"Liars are kicked out of school," snapped

Melinda. She smiled like she loved that rule a lot.

Lamont frowned at Melinda. "Maybe you should be kicked out of school for walking around with all those freckles."

Melinda spun on one foot and marched away. Lucy watched her go.

"Gordie, you can have one of my talents since I have so many. Do you want me to teach you to draw with your eyes closed?"

"No," said Gordie. "Scratch is my talent act."

"Scratch will be the star of the show," added Lamont. "I'm going to go help Gordie with the tricks today after school."

"Hey, Lamont," called Red. He raced over with Mikey and Amon. "Do you want to come over to the television studio with me today?"

Lamont laughed. "Cool. I'll ask my mom."

"We get to come, too," said Mikey.

Red nodded toward Lucy and Gordie. "Next time I'll ask you two to come, but my mom only allows three friends at a time."

"Don't forget to ask me," said Lucy. "Maybe the TV people will want to put me in a commercial."

Gordie shrugged. "I'll probably be too busy teaching Scratch his tricks." He looked over at Lamont, hoping he would remember about their plans to work with Scratch.

But Lamont must have forgotten. Gordie watched as he raced off across the playground with Red and the other boys.

Lucy asked, "Want me to come over and help with Scratch? I love dogs."

Gordie shook his head. "No thanks. I'll get him ready all by myself."

Lucy turned and hurried over to the swing sets.

"Scratch just has to learn two tricks before Friday," muttered Gordie. "Then no one will care about Red's dumb dog."

Gordie smelled peanut butter. He turned around and saw Larry Green. He was stuffing saltine crackers into his mouth.

"Who's Red?" asked Larry. He was in the fourth grade, but he knew kids in every grade. He always ate leftover food from other kids' lunches.

"He's a new kid in our class," said Gordie. "His dog does television commercials. When he brings the dog to the talent show, Red will be the star of third grade."

"What are you going to do for the show?" asked Larry.

"I don't know." Gordie was tired of pretending Scratch knew tricks. Besides, last Sunday Larry had seen a big squirrel chasing Scratch in the park.

"I'd do a back flip," said Larry. "I can do ten in a row."

Gordie dug in his pocket and pulled out a candy bar. "I'll give you this candy bar if you teach me how to do a flip."

"Sure. Come over to the grass." Larry ripped off the wrapper and ate the candy bar in two bites. He handed Gordie the wrapper.

A few fourth-graders came over to watch Larry as he began. Gordie spotted Lamont and Red playing basketball with some fifth-graders. Wait until they saw him doing back flips across the playground.

Gordie felt better already. Once he learned to flip, Scratch could stay home.

Larry stood up and brushed off his pants. "Okay, Gordie, now just put your hands like this. Then make your head look back like this."

Gordie watched Larry do another perfect back flip.

"Okay, Gordie, your turn. Lean your head back and flip."

Larry gave Gordie's back a push. For

one great second, Gordie was in the air. Then he crashed onto his head.

"Good try, kid," said Larry. "Your forehead is grass-stained. Want to try again?"

"No thanks." Gordie brushed the dirt from his hair. What was he going to do now? Gordie rubbed his head. It hurt. Too bad it didn't fall off and roll down the hill. Then Miss Tingle would say he didn't have to be in the show. Then his brother, Doug,

wouldn't be mad when he watched his dumb act.

The recess bell rang. Unless a tornado picked Gordie up and blew him to Ohio, he'd have to teach Scratch a good trick by Friday. And since Lamont was busy with his new best friend, Gordie would have to do it by himself.

Chapter

5

Gordie hopped off the bus. Scratch was busy digging a big hole in Mrs. Yurcon's front yard. Gordie hurried over. Mrs. Yurcon usually turned the hose on Scratch when he started ruining her yard.

"You have the worst-behaved dog in the world," she would shout as Scratch raced around the yard, barking at the hose.

"Come here, boy," called Gordie. He got down on the grass and hugged his dog. "Want to go to school with me on Friday? Want to show my class how smart you are?"

Scratch licked Gordie's ear.

"Lucy has a zillion talents," said Gordie. "And Lamont thinks the new kid in school is real cool. Cooler than me."

"Hey, Shrimp," said Doug. He tapped Gordie on the head with his baseball cap. "Want to go to the park with Miller and me and hit some balls?"

"I have to get ready for the talent show, Doug. I have to teach Scratch two tricks. He's my talent."

Scratch rolled on his back. His four skinny legs waved in the air.

Doug laughed. "Hey, pretty good trick. Use that in the act."

"The tricks have to be hard," explained Gordie. "Hard enough to make the fifth-graders clap."

Doug shook his head. "I don't know, Shrimp. My class didn't even clap when the weather man from channel four came to our room."

Gordie looked down at Scratch as he dug his nose into the grass.

"If I were you, I'd get a new act," said Doug. "Especially since that new kid has a famous dog. I can hardly wait to see him."

For the next ten minutes, Gordie tried

to see how many tricks Scratch knew how to do.

He didn't know how to do any.

Mom came out the back door with peanut butter on crackers. "If you aren't coming inside for your snack, I'd better bring it to you."

"Thanks, Mom." Gordie scrambled up and took a cracker.

Scratch sniffed the air, then charged over, barking. He sat down by Gordie's feet and wagged his tail. Gordie tossed him a tiny bite.

"That dog will do anything for food," said Mom.

"I know," said Gordie. "Especially peanut butter."

Before Mom went inside, she picked up a tennis ball and threw it across the hedge. Scratch took off after the ball. He raced around the side of the house. When Scratch returned, he didn't have the tennis ball in his mouth. He had Mrs. Yurcon's yellow garden gloves. Mrs. Yurcon chased after Scratch.

"Give me back those gloves, you dumb dog," she cried.

"Sorry, Mrs. Yurcon," said Gordie. "I'm teaching him to fetch."

"Teach him some manners instead," she said, and then went back to her yard.

Gordie shook his head. "Now pay attention, Scratch. You have to learn some tricks."

Gordie shared his snack with Scratch and then tried to teach him to roll over. Gordie rolled the dog down the side of the yard. Scratch just waited for Gordie to roll him. No one in room 9 would clap for that trick. Lumpy Labriola would get all the fifth-grade boys to boo.

Gordie sighed and lay down next to his dog. Scratch's tummy growled. Scratch liked food as much as Larry Green.

Gordie stood up fast. He had an idea. Scratch would learn tricks faster with a secret weapon—and the weapon was right inside Gordie's kitchen.

Chapter
6

Gordie raced inside his house and pulled open the pantry door.

"Yippee," he said. He grabbed a large jar of peanut butter and hurried back outside. Scratch was busy chasing the neighbor's cat around the garage.

"Come here, boy," Gordie called. As soon as he took the lid off the peanut butter and waved it around, Scratch came galloping over.

Gordie and Scratch worked hard all afternoon. It took half a jar of peanut butter to teach Scratch two tricks.

After dinner, Gordie showed off his magical dog. "Watch this, Doug. Sit!"

Scratch sat down. Gordie gave his dog

a spoonful of peanut butter. Scratch licked the spoon clean.

"Cool," said Doug.

"Watch this one," said Gordie. "It's harder. Okay, now, speak!"

Scratch barked. Gordie got a new spoon and held out another spoonful of peanut butter.

"What do you think of my act for the talent show, Doug?"

Doug shook his head. "Well, Shrimp. I don't want to burst your bubble, but I don't think it's good enough. You're up against a television dog."

Gordie thumped down the peanut butter jar.

Doug picked up his backpack and pulled out his math book. "Now, if you could teach Scratch how to do my math homework, he'd be the star of the show."

Scratch thumped his tail and laid his head on Doug's knee.

"Sure," Gordie muttered. "Teach Scratch how to add and subtract by Friday. No problem. It took half a jar of peanut butter to teach Scratch two little tricks."

Scratch closed his eyes and whined, like he was sad he knew only dumb tricks.

"You'll think of something," said Doug. "And I'll pay Lumpy not to boo you."

Gordie smiled. He had the best big brother. "Doug, will you clap for me for free?"

"Yeah. I'll get my friends to clap for you, too."

"Thanks." Gordie watched as Doug worked on a math sheet. "Is that hard?" he asked.

"Yeah, it is. I hate to subtract really big numbers."

Gordie loved math. In fact, he loved it so much that he thought it was easy. He sat down and patted Scratch, wondering how hard it would be to teach a dog to add.

"Gordie," Mom called. "Telephone call."

Gordie darted to the phone. "Hello?"

"Gordie, it's me," said Lamont. "Hey, sorry I forgot to come over today."

"That's okay," said Gordie. "I taught Scratch two tricks and—"

"You won't believe how cute Red's dog is," Lamont said. "His dog is named Lawrence. He doesn't have to sleep outside in a doghouse because he has his own bedroom. He has this fluffy cushion and. . . ." Lamont stopped to catch his breath. "Anyway, their house is cool and his mom let us order an extra-large pizza and wings. She said we could order anything we wanted, and we didn't even have a coupon."

Gordie chewed his lip. His mom always made them use coupons for pizza, but she never ordered a pepperoni pizza when Lamont was visiting. Everyone knew Lamont hated pepperoni.

"Red wants to know if I can sleep over at his house on Saturday, but I told him that we were supposed to go fishing with your uncle Leo." Lamont cleared his throat. "So, my mom said I should call you."

Gordie smiled. "Yeah, Uncle Leo said we could bring the tent and sleep out if you want. He'll tell us the best stories about being chased by bears and crazy raccoons—"

Lamont cleared his throat again. "Yeah, well I think I heard those stories last time. So, anyway, Red asked me to sleep over since his dad is taking everyone to Cleveland for a Cavs basketball game and . . ." Lamont was quiet. "So, I guess I can't go fishing with you and Uncle Leo. Is that cool with you?"

Gordie nodded. It took another two seconds before he could make his voice strong enough to say, "Oh, sure."

Chapter
7

By the time Gordie went upstairs to his bedroom, he was more mad than sad. Lamont wasn't a best friend at all. He was a crummy friend. Gordie sat on the side of his bed and wondered who he should ask to go fishing. He'd ask someone right in front of Lamont. He would ask someone in a loud voice and then high-five him. Gordie flopped over on his bed and pulled his pillow over his head.

Doug walked into the room and tossed his backpack into the corner. "Finished my math. Want to go shoot hoops with me?"

"No thanks," Gordie mumbled from underneath the pillow.

Doug pulled the pillow away and

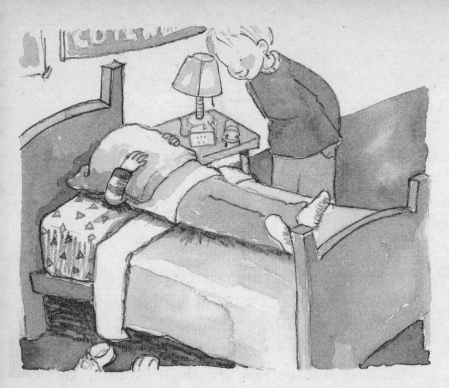

swatted Gordie. "Hey, don't sweat the talent show. You'll think of something."

Gordie sat up. "Sure, all I have to do is teach Scratch how to add and subtract. No problem."

"Gordie Barr!" Mom hollered up the stairs.

Gordie hopped off the bed. Mom only used both names when he was in trouble. "What, Mom?"

Mom walked up the stairs, holding the peanut butter jar. "Did you give Scratch this jar to play with?"

Scratch peeked out from behind Mom's jeans. He had peanut butter smeared all over his whiskers.

"No, I set the jar on the table." Gordie tried not to smile.

Mom tried not to smile back. She handed Gordie the jar. "Here you go. This jar probably has fleas in it. You can use the rest of it to train this silly dog."

Scratch raced into Gordie's room, licking his whiskers. Gordie hurried back into his room and put the peanut butter on his dresser. "Sit, Scratch."

Scratch sat down, his eyes glued to the jar. Gordie paced. There just had to be a way to get Scratch to do a great trick using peanut butter.

Doug held up a deck of cards. "Want to play cards?"

Scratch got up and jumped on Doug's bed, licking the cards. Doug held the deck

up, laughing. "You can't eat the cards, Scratch."

Gordie smiled, then stood frozen in the middle of the room. He looked at the deck of cards and then back to the peanut butter jar.

"I've got it, Doug!" said Gordie. "I think I know how to teach Scratch to do math."

"Then you'll be the star of the show," said Doug. "Scratch will be the smartest dog in the whole world."

Gordie took the cards from Doug and laid them next to the peanut butter. He didn't care if Scratch was the smartest dog in the world. He just had to be better than Red's dog. Gordie picked up the cards and counted them. Fifty-two. Gordie counted out four cards. That was all he would need to make Scratch the star of the third-grade talent show.

Chapter

8

Gordie could hardly wait to get to school. He'd tell Miss Tingle about his new act. Then he'd ask Mikey to go fishing with Uncle Leo. Gordie walked to his locker. Last night he had tried to teach Scratch to add using the playing cards. Scratch was hard to teach. He kept trying to eat the cards. When Gordie lost his temper and said, "Don't eat these, Scratch!" the dog crawled under the bed.

Gordie hung his jacket in his locker. He looked down the hall and saw Red and Lamont laughing by the water fountain. Gordie slammed his locker and walked inside room 9. Just wait until they saw Scratch's trick. The only problem was, the

show was in three days. That didn't leave much time.

As soon as Gordie slid into his seat, Mikey walked in.

"Hey, Mikey, come over here," called Gordie.

"Hi, Gordie. Only three more days till the big show."

Gordie tried not to frown. "Don't remind me. Hey, do you want to go fishing with me and my uncle Leo on Saturday? He's cool and . . ."

Mikey's face got a little red, and he started bending a paper clip back and forth. "Gosh, that sounds fun, but . . ." Mikey looked over his shoulder at Red and Lamont, who were making a lot of noise by the globe. "Red asked me to go to a basketball game in—"

"Cleveland," said Gordie. Was Red's dad taking the whole third grade to the basketball game?

Lamont came over and knocked his knuckles on Gordie's head. "Anybody home?"

Lamont had been knocking on Gordie's head since kindergarten. Gordie usually laughed. But not today.

"Leave me alone," he snapped. He shook Lamont's hand away and opened his desk. He stared inside, wishing a fire alarm would ring so everyone would have to run outside. He would keep on running, straight to his house.

"What a grouch," muttered Lamont. He slid into his own seat.

Once the morning bell rang, Gordie had a hard time concentrating. Miss Tingle was excited about the talent show. She let the whole class skip spelling so they could make tickets for the fifth-graders. Gordie wanted to raise his hand and tell Miss Tingle that he couldn't do the show after all. But he knew she wouldn't believe him. Besides, Gordie had already told a big lie. He had told everyone that his dog knew tricks.

When Miss Tingle announced it was time for lunch, Gordie tapped Lamont on the arm. "Want to eat lunch together?"

Lamont shrugged. "Yeah, sure." Lamont leaned over to Red. "You ready for lunch?"

Red smiled and held up a big paper bag. "I had my mom pack an extra pepperoni and cheese sandwich for you, Lamont."

Gordie waited for Lamont to tell Red that he hated pepperoni. He hated it so much that Gordie never ordered it on his pizza so Lamont wouldn't even have to smell it.

Lamont looked over at Gordie, then turned back to Red. "Great."

Gordie grabbed his bag and hurried to line up. Lamont was busy talking to Red. Lamont was acting like a big faker. Maybe he would go ahead and eat the pepperoni and throw up all over the cafeteria.

"Want to eat lunch together, Mikey?" asked Gordie.

Mikey was busy balancing raisins on his closed eyes, but he said, "Okay."

Lunch wasn't as much fun eating with Mikey. He spent more time playing with his food. He ripped the crust off his bread and then rolled his cheese sandwich into tiny balls.

"Don't they look like snowballs?" asked Mikey as he made a tiny cheese-sandwich snowman.

Gordie kept watching Lamont, waiting for him to throw up. He saw Lamont hide bits of pepperoni inside his lunch bag whenever Red wasn't looking.

By the time school was over, Gordie had a huge headache. His head hurt so much he was afraid it would crack open and his brain would bounce out like a rubber ball. Gordie hopped off the bus. He wasn't looking forward to teaching Scratch math tricks.

When Gordie walked into the kitchen, Scratch was asleep under the table.

"Your dog spent the entire day trying to jump onto your dresser to get to the peanut butter, Gordie," said Mom. She put a plate of sliced apples on the table. "I finally had to close your bedroom door."

"Sorry, Mom."

Gordie handed Mom his math sheet. "I got them all right."

Mom kissed Gordie's head and stuck the

math page onto the refrigerator. "You are such a math whiz."

Doug walked in and tossed his backpack onto the floor. "Is that pizza I smell?"

Mom smiled and opened the oven. "Pepperoni."

"Great!" said Doug.

Gordie stared at the pepperoni and felt bad. He thought of how sick Lamont had looked after lunch. Miss Tingle had told him to go down to the nurse's room and lie on the hard green couch.

"I'm not hungry, Mom," Gordie said as he walked upstairs.

Scratch moaned and followed Gordie up the stairs. The dog slumped down on the floor as Gordie lined up the cards. Gordie held up two cards. "Okay, Scratch. Now pay attention. What do you get when you add the three of clubs to the four of diamonds?"

Scratch leaned over and licked Gordie's sneaker.

"Okay, how about this." Gordie held out the three of clubs and the four of diamonds. "If I add one and two, what do I get?" Gordie held the two cards in front of Scratch's nose.

Scratch licked the four of diamonds.

"No!" cried Gordie. He waved the three of clubs. "It's this one!"

Scratch scrambled to his feet and ran out of the room.

Gordie raced after him. "Sorry, boy. Come back here. I won't yell at you again."

Scratch raced into the bathroom and jumped into the tub.

Gordie skidded to a stop. He really must be a grouch if Scratch would rather have a bath than be with him. Gordie hurried back into his room and stuck his finger in the peanut butter. He went back into the bathroom and let Scratch lick it off. Gordie smiled and held out the two cards. "Now, try again, buddy."

Scratch licked the three of clubs.

"Great!" Gordie hugged his dog. "You did it. Now, try this. What is two and two?"

Scratch licked the three of clubs again.

Gordie tried to keep the smile on his

face. "No, boy. It's the four of diamonds, not the three of clubs. Try again."

Scratch licked the three of clubs and then swallowed it.

"Hey!" Gordie pried open Scratch's mouth and pulled out the card. It was wet and mushy and . . . and it smelled like peanut butter. Gordie smelled his left hand. It still had peanut butter on it. He must have gotten it on the three of clubs and that's why Scratch kept licking it. So if Gordie wanted Scratch to pick a certain card, he just had to use the secret weapon . . . peanut butter.

"Yippee," cried Gordie. He hurried out into the hall and got the rest of the playing cards. "Come on, Scratch. Turning you into a math whiz is going to be a snap. Red's dog is going to look like a kindergarten dog next to you."

Chapter
9

Gordie worked with Scratch every minute he could. It took another jar of peanut butter, but the act was going great. On Friday morning, Gordie could hardly wait to get to school.

Gordie raced into the kitchen. Doug handed him a bagel. "Here, hurry up or we'll miss the bus, Shrimp. Don't want to be late for the big show."

Gordie slid into his seat and drank his juice. "Scratch is going to be great."

"Show me your trick now," said Doug.

Gordie shook his head. "You have to wait. Just make sure your friends clap for me."

"They will. I had to give Lumpy a quarter but Hoover only charged me a dime.

They'll clap real loud. And they won't boo you, not even if you stink."

"Thanks, Doug." Gordie reached down and patted Scratch. "Mom, make sure you don't feed Scratch this morning. He has to be real hungry for the show."

"Aye, aye, sir," said Mom. "I'll even give him a bath." Mom glanced at the clock. "Take the bagels with you, boys. Time to catch the bus. Scratch and I will see you at one o'clock."

Gordie got up and shoved the peanut butter jar and playing cards into his backpack. Scratch got up and sniffed Gordie's backpack, wagging his tail.

"Not now, boy," said Gordie. "It's almost showtime!"

Chapter

10

Lamont wasn't on the bus that morning. Gordie wasn't surprised. Lamont had driven to school with Red's dad for the past three days. Red lived a block away and he said Lamont could ride to school with him so he could sleep an extra twenty minutes.

Gordie leaned against the bus window. He tried not to look sad that he had to sit next to a sixth-grade girl who kept cracking her gum and yelling to her friends two rows back.

When Gordie hurried into room 9, Miss Tingle handed him a cupcake. "Good morning, Gordie. I brought treats since it's our talent-show day. Are you excited?"

"Yes, my mom is giving Scratch a bath so he won't leave fleas in your room."

Miss Tingle patted Gordie's back. "Great. We'll have two dogs in third grade today. Red's mother said Lawrence will be here at one. I hope the dogs get along."

Gordie shrugged. "Scratch loves everyone. Except Mrs. Cillo's cat."

As more and more kids arrived, Gordie started to get nervous. Half of him was excited. The other half was worried that Scratch might not want any peanut butter today. Or he might decide that Lawrence looked like Mrs. Cillo's cat and chase him all over the school.

Lamont rushed in with Red. They were talking about how cool the basketball game was going to be. Gordie didn't care. He was going to have lots of fun fishing. Uncle Leo had said that Gordie could bring Scratch instead of Lamont. Gordie was already planning to bring pepperoni sandwiches for lunch. Maybe fifty. Lamont wouldn't be there to smell them.

When the lunch bell rang in room 9, everyone cheered. Right after lunch, the talent show would get started. Gordie stood in line for lunch by himself. He didn't want to eat with Mikey anymore. Yesterday Mikey had had a cream cheese and olive sandwich. But instead of eating it, Mikey had pasted the little green olive slices all over his face.

"Look, I have the olive pox!" Mikey had yelled.

Today, Gordie didn't care if he ate alone. He wanted to think about his act.

But when Lamont asked, "Want to eat lunch with Red and me?" Gordie said okay.

At lunch Gordie mostly listened to Red brag about things. He bragged ten times more than Lucy. Gordie stared at Lamont, wondering if Lamont still thought Red was cool.

"Wait till you see Lawrence," said Red. "My mom has this leather leash with his initials burned into it. Must have cost a hundred bucks."

Gordie took a tiny bite of baloney and hoped his mom could find Scratch's green leash. Sometimes when she couldn't find it, she just used part of a clothesline.

Instead of room 9's going out for recess, they waited until Miss Tingle came down and got them from the cafeteria. It was finally showtime.

Miss Tingle walked everyone back upstairs and helped kids with their costumes. Lamont ran around the room. He wanted everyone to see his fake mustache.

"Do I look forty years old, Gordie?" asked Lamont.

"You look fifty or sixty," said Gordie. He wondered if he should have a mustache. Maybe not. Scratch might not know it was him. Gordie didn't want his dog barking at him. The fifth-graders might boo.

"Where's Scratch?" Lamont asked.

"He's coming at one o'clock. He needs to rest."

"Gordie, how come you won't tell me about your act? Are you afraid I'll tell Red?"

Gordie shook his head. "No, it's just that I want it to be a surprise. I haven't told anyone."

"But, we're best friends, aren't we?" Lamont's mustache wiggled around like he was upset.

"I guess. I mean, you're Red's best friend now."

Lamont frowned at Gordie. Then he looked over at Red. "He has lots of stuff. His own television and—"

Miss Tingle flashed the lights. "Five more minutes, ladies and gentlemen. Are we ready?"

Gordie slid back into his seat. Lamont hadn't answered Gordie's question. Was Red now Lamont's best friend? He stared up at the clock. His mom would be walking in the door in ten minutes. He hoped Scratch would be hungry.

Lucy skipped over to Gordie's desk. She twirled around. "How do I look?"

"Good," said Gordie. Lucy was wearing a pink ballet dress. She looked like she'd just jumped out of a little jewelry box.

"Lucy, why are you wearing that?" asked Lamont. "I thought you were going to draw a picture with your eyes shut."

"I am," said Lucy. She spun around again. "I am a ballerina girl who can draw."

Miss Tingle clapped her hands. Gordie thought she looked extra pretty. She had more curls on her head.

"I know we are all excited about the show. But sit down now. We want to get ready for our audience to arrive."

Gordie reached under his desk and got his backpack. He reached in and got the playing cards. He hid the peanut butter in his desk. He didn't want anyone to see his secret weapon.

Gordie looked around the room. Everyone was smiling, anxious for the show to begin. Was Gordie the only one in room 9 who wondered if his act would go all right?

Soon the parents started to arrive. Lucy and Billy gave them programs. Gordie knew his act was the seventh. He'd go on after Lamont. Red's dog was going to be last. Miss Tingle was saving him for the big act, like a fireworks display.

The fifth-graders came into the room. Some fifth-graders sat on the radiator until their teacher, Mr. Johnson, yelled at them. Then everyone sat on the floor and tried to be good.

Red's mom arrived with Lawrence. The dog was short, with shiny golden hair. Gordie thought it was a cocker spaniel. Scratch was a little bit cocker spaniel. He was a little bit of a lot of dogs. Lawrence wore a diamond collar. Gordie bit his lip. Scratch's collar was pretty old. It had come for free inside a bag of dog biscuits.

"Wow, cool dog!" said Mikey. "Can I have his autograph?"

Parents and kids laughed. One fifth-grader leaned over and patted Lawrence's leg. The dog jumped back and barked. Red's mom yanked back on the leash, hard.

Gordie leaned back in his seat. Had that hurt the dog? His mom never hurt Scratch.

Not even when he snuck onto the living room couch and drooled.

More and more parents came in and sat on the small chairs in the back. Gordie looked around the room. Doug smiled and gave him the thumbs-up sign. That made Gordie feel a little better. Lumpy looked over at Gordie and held up a quarter.

Lamont's mother came in. She took a picture of Lamont. Then she said, "Gordie, come over here so I can take a picture of you and Lamont." Gordie stood next to Lamont, but he didn't smile. Neither did Lamont. Maybe Lamont was afraid his mustache would fall off. Or, maybe he was mad that Red wasn't in the picture.

Room 9 was getting filled up. There were only two empty chairs in the back. Gordie got up and peeked into the hall. Where was Mom? Where was Scratch?

"Hey, Gordie," whispered Doug. "Where's Mom?"

"I don't know." Gordie looked down at his cards. What if Mom didn't come?

Scratch hated baths. Maybe he'd jumped out of the tub and run off.

Miss Tingle flashed the lights on and off. The show was about to begin.

Gordie kept his head down. Without Scratch, Gordie didn't have an act. And without an act, he'd be kicked out of the show.

Miss Tingle walked to the front of the room. "Thank you for coming to our show."

"You're welcome," called out a fifth-grader.

"We will start our talent show with Lucy Diaz," said Miss Tingle. "Lucy will draw a bird while wearing a blindfold."

Miss Tingle blindfolded Lucy. Then she handed her a big black marker.

Lucy drew a pretty good bird. One eye was not on its head. It floated beside the bird like a little black balloon.

A fifth-grader laughed. Doug leaned over and poked him. Gordie was glad his brother was here.

Gordie looked at the closed door. No Mom. No Scratch.

Billy went next. Then David, Tomeka, and Amy. Finally Miss Tingle called Lamont's name. He played the guitar and sang. The fifth-graders whistled and clapped.

Gordie's hands started to sweat. He was next! Maybe he could tell Miss Tingle he had to throw up. She would send him to the nurse's room, and he could lie on the couch until the show was over.

Gordie's heart was pounding so hard he was sure everyone could hear it. He was about to cover his ears when the door to room 9 opened.

Chapter
11

Scratch burst into the room, pulling Gordie's mom with him.

"Hey, Doug, your dog's taking your mom for a walk," Lumpy called out.

When Scratch heard Doug's name, his head jerked up and he tried to pull Mom through the crowd. Mom dug her heels down and held tightly.

"Is that the TV star?" asked a fifth-grader.

"No," said her friend. "That's just a regular old dog."

Scratch sat down and scratched behind his left ear.

"Fleabag," whispered a fifth-grader.

Gordie was glad when Doug leaned over and shushed the kid.

"Sorry, Miss Tingle," said Mom. "When I got to school, Scratch jumped out and a squirrel chased him."

"Maybe your dog is a chicken instead of a dog," said Red.

"Settle down, please," said Miss Tingle. "Gordie and his dog will be next."

Gordie stood up. He put his playing cards in one hand and walked to the front of the room. Scratch licked Gordie's hand and followed him. Gordie bowed. He pointed to Scratch. "Today you will meet the smartest dog in the world."

"If he's so smart, what's the capital of Ohio?" called out Lucy.

Lots of kids laughed. Lamont clapped and nodded his head.

"Let's give Gordie our attention," said Miss Tingle.

Gordie nodded and started his act. "Sit, Scratch." Scratch sat down. He was staring at the playing cards. His tongue hung out.

Gordie pulled the cards from his pocket. He held them up in the air. "My dog will now answer an addition problem."

Gordie walked to the board. He printed: $4+3=$___.

"Okay, Scratch. Four plus three equals what?" Gordie held the playing cards up again. "I have a seven of hearts and a three of clubs. Which is it, Scratch?"

Scratch sniffed both cards. Then he licked the seven of hearts.

Gordie held up the seven of hearts. Everyone clapped.

"Now for the hard question," said Gordie. "Only a few dogs in the world can do subtraction." Gordie printed: $12-5=$___ on the board. "Twelve minus five is what, Scratch?"

Scratch sniffed both cards. Then he licked the seven of hearts. He licked it again, and then bit down hard on it.

Gordie pulled it from Scratch's mouth. He held the wet card up in the air.

"Yes, twelve minus five equals seven."

Everyone clapped. A few fifth-graders whistled. Gordie found Doug in the crowd. He gave Gordie the thumbs-up sign.

"How'd you do that?" asked Lucy. "Let me see those cards!"

Gordie's hand closed around the playing cards. He didn't want Lucy to discover his secret weapon.

"Your dog isn't that smart," said Red. "He's only doing second-grade math."

"Yeah," added Lumpy. "It's not like Scratch knows how to read."

A few kids laughed, but they stopped right away when Mr. Johnson stood up and frowned at Lumpy.

"Scratch loves to read," Gordie said slowly. It was true, sort of. Whenever Gordie read aloud, Scratch would lie down beside him, like he was listening. Gordie smiled, remembering how Scratch thumped his tail when Gordie changed his voice as he read.

Miss Tingle smiled at Gordie. "Does Scratch have a favorite story?"

Gordie tried to think fast. Everyone was watching him.

"Dogs can't read," muttered Red.

Gordie patted the dog's head. Scratch wasn't the smartest dog in the world, but he wasn't a dope, either.

Dope . . . dopey. Gordie smiled. He knew what he would say.

"Scratch loves *Snow White,* Miss Tingle. He knows all about that book."

Miss Tingle looked surprised. "He does?"

"Sure," Gordie said. "And he can prove it."

"No dog can understand a book," said Red.

"Scratch can," said Gordie. He cleared his throat and led Scratch back to the chalkboard. "My dog needs his own library card."

Lots of kids laughed.

"Sure . . ." Gordie's hand closed around his cards. "Scratch, remember how much you liked *Snow White*?"

Scratch sat down and scratched behind his left ear.

Red shook his head. "Yeah, right."

Gordie held out both playing cards. "How many dwarves did Snow White live with, Scratch?"

Gordie pushed the cards closer to Scratch. Come on, boy, thought Gordie. You can do it.

"I know how many," said a tall fifth-grade girl with red hair. "I can name them all. There's Bashful and Happy and—"

Miss Tingle held up her hand. "Let Scratch answer."

"How many dwarves?" Gordie asked quietly.

Scratch lowered his head and then licked the seven of hearts.

"Way to go, Scratch," called Doug.

"Nice trick," added Mr. Johnson. When he started clapping, the rest of the audience joined in. When Lumpy whistled, no one even yelled at him.

"Good job, Gordie," said Miss Tingle. "Take a bow!"

As Gordie bent down, Scratch reached over and grabbed the seven of hearts. With one chomp, the card disappeared.

Gordie tried not to laugh. Now nobody would discover the peanut butter smeared on the back of the card.

"Wow!" said Miss Tingle. "Scratch is quite a dog. He made the card disappear! Scratch knows math and magic."

"I love your magic dog," Lucy called out.

Gordie put Scratch on his leash and they sat down and watched the rest of the show. During the next act, Scratch yawned and fell asleep. Gordie kept his arm around him and watched the show.

Miss Tingle clapped after Mikey played "Jingle Bells" using only his nose. "Now, we are all very lucky to have a chance to meet Lawrence, the television dog."

Gordie watched as the fifth-graders got real quiet.

Red got out of his seat and took the leather leash from his mother.

"Come on, boy," said Red. The dog trotted after Red to the center of the room. "My dog is going to sit, kneel, roll over, and then do a flip in the air."

Lumpy Labriola whistled twice. Then his teacher leaned over and said something loudly in his ear.

"My dog is used to being around professionals, so please try not to get yelled at during his act," said Red. "And don't take flash pictures."

Mr. Johnson lowered his camera and frowned at Red.

Gordie leaned forward and watched as Lawrence sat, knelt, rolled over, and then stood up, ready for the flip.

"Try to remain quiet," said Red. He looked stern.

Mr. Johnson stood up and snapped his fingers at his class. "I don't want to hear a word. Pay attention." He gave one final snap. Everyone sat up straighter, even the adults.

Lawrence swung his sleek head toward Mr. Johnson. He sat down and hung his head.

Red jerked on Lawrence's leash. The dog's head swung up, then struggled against the leash.

Red's mother leaned over and swatted the dog under its chin. The kids in the room started to squirm. Red's cheeks got pink.

"Why do they hit the dog?" whispered Lamont.

"He usually doesn't do this," said Red's mother. "The dog is a professional."

Scratch scrambled to his feet, wagging his tail.

Gordie watched as Red and his mother tried to calm down Lawrence. The dog was prancing around in a tiny circle, pulling on his leash. A few of the fifth-graders started to laugh.

"Class, let's settle down," said Miss Tingle. She looked at the light switch like she wanted to flash the lights.

"Can I start my act over?" asked Red.

"I feel sick," called out Mikey.

Lawrence started barking at Mikey. Red jerked the leash. Gordie was out of his seat before he knew it. He had the jar of peanut butter in his hand. "Here, Red. Offer your dog some of this. Scratch loves it."

Red stared at Gordie. "Peanut butter?"

Gordie nodded, scooping out a finger-ful and offering it to Lawrence. Lawrence backed away, then sat down. Gordie leaned closer. Red patted Lawrence on the head. "Go on, boy. I love peanut butter, too."

Lawrence looked up at Red, then gently licked the peanut butter from Gordie's fin-ger. Scratch scurried up the aisle, sniffing the air. Doug hopped up and tried to grab Scratch. But Scratch raced over to Lawrence, his tail going faster than wind-shield wipers.

"Get your dog away from Lawrence," snapped Red.

"It's okay. Scratch loves everyone," said Gordie. "Except squirrels and Mrs. Cillo's cat."

Red shook his head. "I don't know. . . ."

Gordie patted Scratch. "Sit down, Scratch."

Scratch sat, then he stuck out his long tongue and licked a small bit of peanut but-ter from Lawrence's face.

Lawrence blinked, then slid down and rolled over.

The entire room started to laugh. Miss Tingle started to clap and then everyone joined in. Lumpy stood up and whistled.

Gordie pulled Scratch back and hugged him. Red smiled at Gordie and then knelt down and hugged Lawrence, too.

When everyone stopped clapping, Lucy stood up. "Since Gordie got two turns, can I do a second act?"

"Sure, Lucy, go ahead," called out Lamont. "Gordie and I are still waiting for you to disappear."

Lucy shook her fist at Lamont, but she was smiling. Gordie stood up and clapped his hands. Scratch followed him back to his seat.

"Man, Scratch is the coolest dog in the world," said Lamont. He raised his hand halfway up for a high five, but then he stopped.

"You're not so bad yourself," said Gordie. He kept one hand on Scratch's head and with the other he met Lamont's in a loud high five. Scratch sat down and thumped his tail.

Miss Tingle thanked everyone for coming and then took the wrap off a huge sheet cake. Lamont's mom served punch in paper cups. The fifth-grade teacher, Mr. Johnson, allowed the fifth-graders to play hangman on the board with the third-graders.

Red walked back to Gordie's desk.

"Thanks for the peanut butter, Gordie," said Red. "I don't know why Lawrence got stage fright. He's used to being in front of lights and cameras."

"But not lots of fifth-graders," added Lamont. "Scratch is used to them because of Gordie's brother, Doug."

Red grinned. "Looks like our dogs like each other."

"Yeah." Gordie kept his face against Scratch's head. Why did he feel so mean all of a sudden? It was probably because Scratch liked Lawrence, but Gordie didn't like Red. Maybe it was easier for dogs to be nice.

Gordie and Red waited by the chalkboard with their dogs while the fifth-graders filed out of room 9.

"Fifth-graders, quiet in the hall," announced Mr. Johnson. As he passed the dogs, he gave them each a pat on the head. "Nice job, boys."

Gordie wasn't sure if Mr. Johnson was talking to them or the dogs.

Red handed Gordie the peanut butter. "Thanks, Gordie. I won't tell anyone about the secret weapon. Not even Lamont."

Gordie looked over at Lamont. Lamont gave him a thumbs-up sign. "That's okay. You can tell Lamont. He's . . . he's my best friend."

Red nodded. "I know. He told me that about ten times."

"He did?" Gordie smiled.

"I had a best friend at my old school," said Red. "Jack is really funny."

"Maybe he can come and visit you sometime," said Gordie.

"Maybe," said Red. But he sounded like Jack wouldn't visit.

"Lawrence has an audition at the television studio," said Red's mom.

Red handed the leash to his mother. "Thanks, Mom."

After Red's dog left, Gordie walked back to his seat. Lamont had his hand up in the air. "Way to go, Gordie. Slap me five."

Gordie and Lamont high-fived.

Lamont sniffed his hand. "Hey, I smell like peanut butter."

Gordie sniffed his own hand and laughed.

"I guess this makes us peanut-butter blood brothers," said Lamont. He looked up at Gordie and grinned.

Gordie grinned back. "Peanut-butter blood brothers best friends."

Gordie held up his hand and Lamont met his with the loudest high-five of all.